This book belongs to

....

For my family, whose love and help have brought me here

A Random House book
Published by Random House Australia Pty Ltd
Level 3, 100 Pacific Highway, North Sydney NSW 2060
www.randomhouse.com.au

First published by Random House Australia in 2010

Addresses for companies within the Random House Group can be found at www.randomhouse.com.au/offices.

National Library of Australia
Cataloguing-in-Publication Entry

       Author: Pelling, Lenny
       Title: School days / Lenny Pelling
       ISBN: 978 1 86471 901 7 (pbk.)
       Series: Pen pals forever; 2
       Target audience: For pre-school age
       Dewey number: A823.3

Cover and internal illustration by Lenny Pelling
Cover design by Leanne Beattie
Internal design and typesetting by Astred Hicks, designcherry
Printed in Australia by The SOS Print + Media Group

10 9 8 7 6 5 4 3 2

LENNY PELLING

Pen Pals

FOREVER

School Days

RANDOM HOUSE AUSTRALIA

Polly's summer adventures travelling
with her grandparents had been so
much fun. But it was lucky they were

over now, because the tiny caravan
could barely hold her collection
of scrapbooks.

Jez's stack of shoeboxes was
beginning to get in the way too.

Their letters, postcards and photos
were taking up more space than
either of the girls had room for.

This year, Polly and Jez were both
starting at new schools and they
would need space for workbooks,
art projects and . . . homework.

For Polly, school would be very
different this year.

Her parents were travelling for work,
and Great-auntie Meryl needed a
hand to run her sheep farm, Glossop

8

Downs. Polly, Gran and Pop would
live there for a while, and Polly
would go to school over the internet.

At lunchtime, Polly would have the
whole farm as her playground.

Jez's new school would be much
bigger than her old one.

The week before term began, Jez and
her mum went shopping for her new
uniform. It was tight and scratchy and
not at all what she had been used to
at her old school. And with so many
kids, how would her mum find Jez at
the school gate?

According to her teacher, Polly's classroom was the biggest in the whole country. Like Polly, kids from miles around would be sitting at their kitchen tables.

Polly wondered if other kids had to help with rounding up sheep and making meals for the shearers, on top of going to school.

Jez thought her classroom could be a little larger. She wondered if the other kids would like her.

15

Polly was going to be busy this year!
How would she find time to write
to Jez?

Jez might have
plenty of time for
postcards . . . but
would she have
anything to write?

Dear Polly,

Today was my first day. I have to sit next to Billy Fletcher, the most talkative boy in school. At recess he told jokes with a mouthful of ham sandwich. At lunchtime, he told stories while he beat the other boys at handball. I could still hear him talking when I got home from school.

Love from your friend Jez

Polly thought her classmates were a little noisy, too.

Dear Polly,

Do you still get homework when you go to school at home? There seems to be almost as much to do after school as when I'm there. Miss Milligan wants me to write a story. She said I could use my letters to you, but I have to imagine you are a princess, or a monster, or a desert explorer.

Love Jez

Polly set out on an expedition to discover the rare and dangerous woolly Merino.

Dear Polly,

I don't think I like school much. Today, Billy Fletcher dared me to quack like a duck in class. I said I would if he would moo like a cow at lunch. Billy didn't have to say moo even once, because I spent lunchtime writing lines for Miss Milligan.

Love Jez

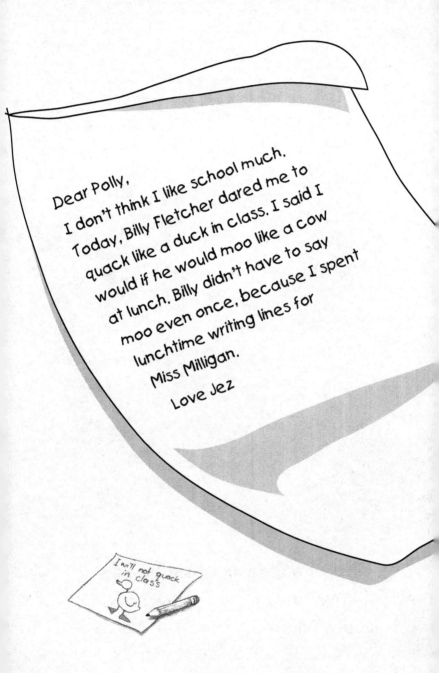

As hard as she tried, Polly just
couldn't work out how to talk
to sheep.

Dear Polly,

I know what I want to do when I grow up! We went on an excursion to the zoo yesterday and I got to hold a lizard. I fed it black beetles like the ones on Mrs Formby's azaleas. She spends hours picking off every single one when all she really needs is a crested iguana.

Love, Zookeeper Jez

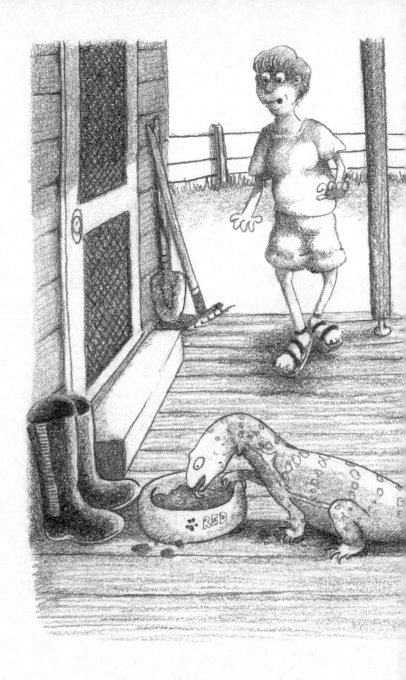

Polly and her gran learned a lot about
what lizards like for dinner.

Dearest Polly,

It has been raining here all week and we can't go out at lunchtime. Sometimes we watch movies or play cards. Peter Finnegan fell asleep halfway through a game of snap, and there is so much water in the sand pit that it looks like the bottom of the sea.

Love Jez

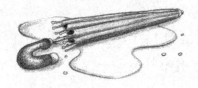

Polly's Auntie Meryl couldn't
remember the last time it had rained.

Dear Polly,

I made a friend today. Her name is Lisa. She's new to this school too. In fact, her family has only been in Australia for a year. At home, after she does her homework Lisa teaches her mum to speak English. Lisa's mum taught us how to make dumplings in chicken soup.

Love Jez

Polly taught Red the Kelpie a new trick for show-and-tell.

The text visible on the laptop screen reads: "WOW POLLY! THAT'S AMAZING ☺"

Dear Polly,

This week we did bush dancing in sport. My partner was Amelia Willis because there weren't enough boys to go around. We did the Shearer's Waltz and the Canadian Three Step. Mr Fitzgibbon called the dances like he does every Friday at the footy club. It was great fun!

Love Jez

44

This time, Polly didn't have to
imagine what it would be like to
swap places with Jez.

Dear Polly,

Tomorrow is career costume day at school. At first I wanted to be a wizard but Mum said that wasn't really a job, more of a hobby. In the end, Mum found my costume in the 2-for-1 foil sale at the corner shop.

Love, Outer Space Jez

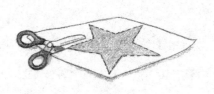

Polly and Pop travelled to a faraway
galaxy every time Gran wanted honey
on her toast.

Dear Polly,

Last night was Parent/Teacher Night at school. I read out my story about a great outback explorer I know. Her name is Polly and she discovered the great plains of Glossop Downs.

Amelia and Lisa showed everyone their volcano made out of macaroni and tomato sauce.

Love Jez

At Polly's Parent/Teacher Night,
everyone crowded around the
kitchen table.

By the end of the term,
Polly had learned that
sometimes it doesn't rain for
years. That sheep are grumpy
and school doesn't have to be held
in a classroom.

Jez had learned more than writing
and maths. She had travelled to the
moon in her home-made rocket. She
had made friends, danced waltzes and
grown up a lot. But she still missed
her best friend Polly.

They would both have to make more room for postcards.

PEN PAL TIPS

Make a rocket with Jez

You will need:

★ 2 pieces of cardboard
★ Scissors
★ Sticky tape
★ Foil
★ Glue
★ Stapler
★ Ribbon
★ Paint and brush

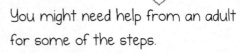

You might need help from an adult for some of the steps.

✦ Step 1

Cut out a circle and a long strip of cardboard.

Make the long strip into a ring that fits your head.

Roll the circle into a cone shape so that it sits on top of the ring.

✦ Step 2

Stick the two hat pieces together.

Glue foil on the outside.

✦ Step 3

Make a wide cardboard cylinder that fits around your tummy.

Cover with foil, just like the hat.

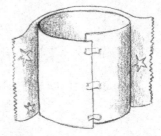

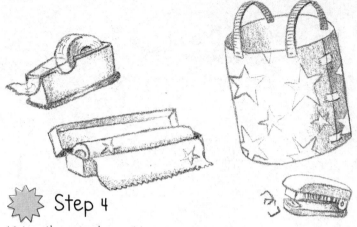

⭐ Step 4

Using the stapler, add some ribbon straps to the cylinder for your shoulders. Add two more to the hat to tie under your chin.

Paint on some stars and . . .

WHOOSH!

You're off to outer space, just like Jez.

PEN PAL TIPS

Write a postcard from space

If you could choose anywhere in the whole universe, where would you go?

Would you ride a comet or chase a star? Would you get lonely?

Would you make friends with an alien?

Would you get cold on the moon?

Make your own postcard! On a piece of cardboard, draw your space trip.

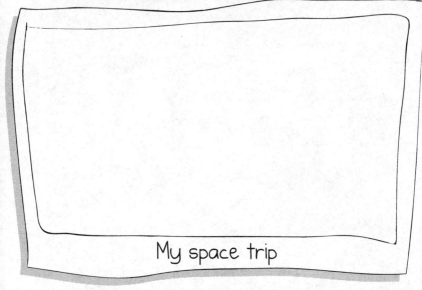

My space trip

On the back, write a postcard from outer space.

Dear

Add a stamp here

Write the address here